Maid

Of

Honor

Important Dates

The Big Day _____

Bridal Shower _____

Bachelorette Party _____

Dress Shopping _____

Dress Alterations _____

Order Attire _____

Rehearsal Dinner _____

Brides Must Haves

To Do List

_____

_____

_____

_____

_____

_____

_____

_____

_____

_____

_____

_____

_____

_____

_____

_____

_____

_____

_____

_____

_____

_____

_____

_____

_____

_____

_____

_____

Wedding Day Emergency Kit

1. Sewing kit
2. Clear nail polish and super glue
3. Bottle of water
4. Snacks
5. Bobby pins/ Hair ties
6. Hairspray
7. Lipstick
8. Tissues
9. OTC Pain med
10. Small mirror
11. Deodorant
12. Lint brush
13. Flip flops
14. Q-Tips
15. Hand wipes

12 Months Before

-Determine your budget
-Make a guest list
-Hire a wedding planner
-Select venue
-Select caterer

11 Months Before

-Choose color theme
-Book Band/D.J,

Photographer/Videographer

10 Months Before

-Shop for your Wedding Dress
-Create a Wedding Website
-Take Engagement photos
-Shop for invitations

9 Months Before

-Purchase Bridal attire
-Mail save-the-date postcards.

8 Months Before

-Start your gift registry
-Select Bridesmaid dresses
-Meet with your florist

7 Months Before

-Book Rehearsal Dinner
-Order any rental items
-Hire an officiant

5 Months Before

-Book transportation
-Book Honeymoon
-Purchase/Rent Grooms'
    Attire

4 Months Before

-Have final tasting
-Choose your cake
-Buy Wedding bands
-Hair and Make-up trial

3 Months Before

-Order favors
-Order invitations and
    Thank-You cards
-Plan dinner menu
-Meet with Officiant
-Write/Choose vows

2 Months Before

-Mail invitations
-Send rehearsal dinner
  invitations
-First dress fitting
-Apply for Marriage license
-Purchase Wedding party
  gifts
-Choose floral arrangements
-Give song selection to
  D.J./Band

1 Month Before

-Assemble gift bags or favors
-Pay vendors
-Create seating chart
-Make place cards
-Have final venue walk
  though
-Break in wedding shoes

<u>Final Week</u>

- Deliver final head count

Pamper Yourself!!!

-Waxing
-Manicure and Pedicure
-Massage

Take a deep breath!!!

The Big Day

-Eat a good breakfast
-Don't sweat the small stuff
-Remember to soak in the
    moment
-Focus on what really matters
-Keep drinks to a minimum
-Remember to delegate
-Take some time alone

Bridesmaids

Name _____

Address _____

_____

Phone _____

E-Mail _____

Name _____

Address _____

_____

Phone _____

E-Mail _____

Name _____

Address _____

_____

Phone _____

E-Mail _____

Bridesmaids

Name _____

Address _____

_____

Phone _____

E-Mail _____

Name _____

Address _____

_____

Phone _____

E-Mail _____

Name _____

Address _____

_____

Phone _____

E-Mail _____

Bridesmaids

Name _____

Address _____

_____

Phone _____

E-Mail _____

Name _____

Address _____

_____

Phone _____

E-Mail _____

Name _____

Address _____

_____

Phone _____

E-Mail _____

Bridesmaids

Name _____

Address _____

_____

Phone _____

E-Mail _____

Name _____

Address _____

_____

Phone _____

E-Mail _____

Name _____

Address _____

_____

Phone _____

E-Mail _____

Month Of

Sunday	Monday	Tuesday	Wednesday	Thursday	Friday	Saturday
☐	☐	☐	☐	☐	☐	☐
☐	☐	☐	☐	☐	☐	☐
☐	☐	☐	☐	☐	☐	☐
☐	☐	☐	☐	☐	☐	☐
☐	☐	☐	☐	☐	☐	☐

Month Of

Sunday	Monday	Tuesday	Wednesday	Thursday	Friday	Saturday
☐	☐	☐	☐	☐	☐	☐
☐	☐	☐	☐	☐	☐	☐
☐	☐	☐	☐	☐	☐	☐
☐	☐	☐	☐	☐	☐	
☐	☐	☐	☐	☐	☐	

Month Of ———

Sunday	Monday	Tuesday	Wednesday	Thursday	Friday	Saturday
☐	☐	☐	☐	☐	☐	☐
☐	☐	☐	☐	☐	☐	☐
☐	☐	☐	☐	☐	☐	☐
☐	☐	☐	☐	☐	☐	☐
☐	☐	☐	☐	☐	☐	☐

Month Of ———

Sunday	Monday	Tuesday	Wednesday	Thursday	Friday	Saturday
☐	☐	☐	☐	☐	☐	☐
☐	☐	☐	☐	☐	☐	☐
☐	☐	☐	☐	☐	☐	☐
☐	☐	☐	☐	☐	☐	☐
☐	☐	☐	☐	☐	☐	☐

Month Of ————

Sunday	Monday	Tuesday	Wednesday	Thursday	Friday	Saturday
☐	☐	☐	☐	☐	☐	☐
☐	☐	☐	☐	☐	☐	☐
☐	☐	☐	☐	☐	☐	☐
☐	☐	☐	☐	☐	☐	☐
☐	☐	☐	☐	☐	☐	☐

Month Of

Sunday	Monday	Tuesday	Wednesday	Thursday	Friday	Saturday
☐	☐	☐	☐	☐	☐	☐
☐	☐	☐	☐	☐	☐	☐
☐	☐	☐	☐	☐	☐	☐
☐	☐	☐	☐	☐	☐	☐
☐	☐	☐	☐	☐	☐	☐

Month Of ──────────

Sunday	Monday	Tuesday	Wednesday	Thursday	Friday	Saturday
☐	☐	☐	☐	☐	☐	☐
☐	☐	☐	☐	☐	☐	☐
☐	☐	☐	☐	☐	☐	☐
☐	☐	☐	☐	☐	☐	☐
☐	☐	☐	☐	☐	☐	☐

Month Of ——————

Sunday	Monday	Tuesday	Wednesday	Thursday	Friday	Saturday
☐	☐	☐	☐	☐	☐	☐
☐	☐	☐	☐	☐	☐	☐
☐	☐	☐	☐	☐	☐	
☐	☐	☐	☐	☐	☐	
☐	☐	☐	☐	☐	☐	

Month Of ——————

Sunday	Monday	Tuesday	Wednesday	Thursday	Friday	Saturday
☐	☐	☐	☐	☐	☐	☐
☐	☐	☐	☐	☐	☐	☐
☐	☐	☐	☐	☐	☐	☐
☐	☐	☐	☐	☐	☐	☐
☐	☐	☐	☐	☐	☐	☐

Month Of ——————

Sunday	Monday	Tuesday	Wednesday	Thursday	Friday	Saturday
☐	☐	☐	☐	☐	☐	☐
☐	☐	☐	☐	☐	☐	☐
☐	☐	☐	☐	☐	☐	☐
☐	☐	☐	☐	☐	☐	☐
☐	☐	☐	☐	☐	☐	☐

Month Of

Sunday	Monday	Tuesday	Wednesday	Thursday	Friday	Saturday

Month Of

Sunday	Monday	Tuesday	Wednesday	Thursday	Friday	Saturday
☐	☐	☐	☐	☐	☐	☐
☐	☐	☐	☐	☐	☐	☐
☐	☐	☐	☐	☐	☐	☐
☐	☐	☐	☐	☐	☐	☐
☐	☐	☐	☐	☐	☐	☐

Bridal Party Planner

Date:

Venue:

Time:

Notes

_____
_____
_____
_____
_____
_____
_____
_____
_____
_____
_____
_____
_____
_____
_____
_____
_____
_____

Notes/Memories

Notes/Memories

Notes/Memories

Notes/Memories

Bridal Party Checklist

- ☐ Pick a date
- ☐ Choose theme
- ☐ Set budget
- ☐ Pick a venue
- ☐ Plan guest list
- ☐ Make reservations
- ☐ Choose caterer
- ☐ Mail invitations
- ☐ Purchase favors
- ☐ Choose games

Budget

Item	Budgeted	Actual

Budget

Item	Budgeted	Actual

Vendor Contacts

Name _____

Address _____

_____

Phone _____

Website _____

Name _____

Address _____

_____

Phone _____

Website _____

Name _____

Address _____

_____

Phone _____

Website _____

Vendor Contacts

Name _____
Address _____
_____

Phone _____
Website _____

Name _____
Address _____
_____

Phone _____
Website _____

Name _____
Address _____
_____

Phone _____
Website _____

Vendor Contacts

Name _____
Address _____

_____

Phone _____
Website _____

Name _____
Address _____

_____

Phone _____
Website _____

Name _____
Address _____

_____

Phone _____
Website _____

Bridal Party Guest List

Name _____
Address _____
_____
Phone _____
E-Mail _____

Name _____
Address _____
_____
Phone _____
E-Mail _____

Name _____
Address _____
_____
Phone _____
E-Mail _____

Bridal Party Guest List

Name _____

Address _____

_____

Phone _____

E-Mail _____

Name _____

Address _____

_____

Phone _____

E-Mail _____

Name _____

Address _____

_____

Phone _____

E-Mail _____

Bridal Party Guest List

Name _____

Address _____

_____

Phone _____

E-Mail _____

Name _____

Address _____

_____

Phone _____

E-Mail _____

Name _____

Address _____

_____

Phone _____

E-Mail _____

Bridal Party Guest List

Name   _____
Address _____

        _____

Phone   _____
E-Mail   _____

Name   _____
Address _____

        _____

Phone   _____
E-Mail   _____

Name   _____
Address _____

        _____

Phone   _____
E-Mail   _____

Bridal Party Guest List

Name _____

Address _____

_____

Phone _____

E-Mail _____

Name _____

Address _____

_____

Phone _____

E-Mail _____

Name _____

Address _____

_____

Phone _____

E-Mail _____

Bridal Party Guest List

Name _____
Address _____
_____

Phone _____
E-Mail _____

Name _____
Address _____
_____

Phone _____
E-Mail _____

Name _____
Address _____
_____

Phone _____
E-Mail _____

Bridal Party Guest List

Name _____

Address _____

_____

Phone _____

E-Mail _____

Name _____

Address _____

_____

Phone _____

E-Mail _____

Name _____

Address _____

_____

Phone _____

E-Mail _____

Bridal Party Guest List

Name _____

Address _____

_____

Phone _____

E-Mail _____

Name _____

Address _____

_____

Phone _____

E-Mail _____

Name _____

Address _____

_____

Phone _____

E-Mail _____

Bridal Party Guest List

Name
_____

Address
_____

_____

Phone
_____

E-Mail
_____

Name
_____

Address
_____

_____

Phone
_____

E-Mail
_____

Name
_____

Address
_____

_____

Phone
_____

E-Mail
_____

Bridal Party Guest List

Name _____

Address _____

_____

Phone _____

E-Mail _____

Name _____

Address _____

_____

Phone _____

E-Mail _____

Name _____

Address _____

_____

Phone _____

E-Mail _____

Bridal Party Guest List

Name _____

Address _____

_____

Phone _____

E-Mail _____

Name _____

Address _____

_____

Phone _____

E-Mail _____

Name _____

Address _____

_____

Phone _____

E-Mail _____

Bridal Party Guest List

Name _____

Address _____

_____

Phone _____

E-Mail _____

Name _____

Address _____

_____

Phone _____

E-Mail _____

Name _____

Address _____

_____

Phone _____

E-Mail _____

Bridal Party Guest List

Name
_____

Address
_____

_____

Phone
_____

E-Mail
_____

Name
_____

Address
_____

_____

Phone
_____

E-Mail
_____

Name
_____

Address
_____

_____

Phone
_____

E-Mail
_____

Bridal Party Guest List

Name _____

Address _____

_____

Phone _____

E-Mail _____

Name _____

Address _____

_____

Phone _____

E-Mail _____

Name _____

Address _____

_____

Phone _____

E-Mail _____

Bridal Party Guest List

Name _____

Address _____

_____

Phone _____

E-Mail _____

Name _____

Address _____

_____

Phone _____

E-Mail _____

Name _____

Address _____

_____

Phone _____

E-Mail _____

Bridal Party Guest List

Name _____

Address _____

_____

Phone _____

E-Mail _____

Name _____

Address _____

_____

Phone _____

E-Mail _____

Name _____

Address _____

_____

Phone _____

E-Mail _____

Bridal Party Guest List

Name _____

Address _____

_____

Phone _____

E-Mail _____

Name _____

Address _____

_____

Phone _____

E-Mail _____

Name _____

Address _____

_____

Phone _____

E-Mail _____

Bridal Party Guest List

Name _____
Address _____

_____

Phone _____
E-Mail _____

Name _____
Address _____

_____

Phone _____
E-Mail _____

Name _____
Address _____

_____

Phone _____
E-Mail _____

Bridal Party Guest List

Name _____

Address _____

_____

Phone _____

E-Mail _____

Name _____

Address _____

_____

Phone _____

E-Mail _____

Name _____

Address _____

_____

Phone _____

E-Mail _____

Bridal Party Guest List

Name _____

Address _____

_____

Phone _____

E-Mail _____

Name _____

Address _____

_____

Phone _____

E-Mail _____

Name _____

Address _____

_____

Phone _____

E-Mail _____

Bridal Party Guest List

Name _____

Address _____

_____

Phone _____

E-Mail _____

Name _____

Address _____

_____

Phone _____

E-Mail _____

Name _____

Address _____

_____

Phone _____

E-Mail _____

Bridal Party Games Ideas

1. He Said, She Said

2. Find the guest

3. Where were we?

4. Who makes the best cocktail?

5. Wedding word scramble

6. Purse scavenger hunt

7. Bride and Groom trivia

8. Whose memory

9. Pin a mustache on the groom

10. Musical Bouquet

Notes/Memories

Helping Hands

Who	What	When

Helping Hands

Who	What	When

Seating Plan

Table

Table

Seating Plan

Table

Table

Seating Plan

Table

Table

Seating Plan

Table

Table

Seating Plan

Table

Table

<u>Seating Plan</u>

Table

Table

<u>Seating Plan</u>

Table

Table

Seating Plan

Table

Table

Seating Plan

Table

Table

Seating Plan

Table

Table

Bachelorette Party

Date:

Venue:

Time:

Notes

_____
_____
_____
_____
_____
_____
_____
_____
_____
_____
_____
_____
_____
_____
_____
_____
_____
_____

Bachelorette Party Checklist

- [ ] Pick a date
- [ ] Pick a theme
- [ ] Set budget
- [ ] Pick a venue
- [ ] Send out invites
- [ ] Pick a menu
- [ ] Buy supplies
- [ ] Choose games
- [ ] Make reservations

Bachelorette Party Games

1. The Groom quiz
2. Scavenger hunt
3. Lingerie shower bingo
4. Ring toss
5. How well do you know the Bachelorette?
6. Ring Hunt
7. Swing your ding a ling
8. I dare you
9. Man hunt
0. Guess the panties

Notes/Memories

Bachelorette Party Guest List

Name _____
Address _____

_____

Phone _____
E-Mail _____

Name _____
Address _____

_____

Phone _____
E-Mail _____

Name _____
Address _____

_____

Phone _____
E-Mail _____

Bachelorette Party Guest List

Name _____

Address _____

_____

Phone _____

E-Mail _____

Name _____

Address _____

_____

Phone _____

E-Mail _____

Name _____

Address _____

_____

Phone _____

E-Mail _____

Bachelorette Party Guest List

Name _____

Address _____

_____

Phone _____

E-Mail _____

Name _____

Address _____

_____

Phone _____

E-Mail _____

Name _____

Address _____

_____

Phone _____

E-Mail _____

Bachelorette Party Guest List

Name _____

Address _____

_____

Phone _____

E-Mail _____

Name _____

Address _____

_____

Phone _____

E-Mail _____

Name _____

Address _____

_____

Phone _____

E-Mail _____

Bachelorette Party Guest List

Name _____

Address _____

_____

Phone _____

E-Mail _____

Name _____

Address _____

_____

Phone _____

E-Mail _____

Name _____

Address _____

_____

Phone _____

E-Mail _____

Bachelorette Party Guest List

Name _____

Address _____

_____

Phone _____

E-Mail _____

Name _____

Address _____

_____

Phone _____

E-Mail _____

Name _____

Address _____

_____

Phone _____

E-Mail _____

Notes/Memories

Notes/Memories

Notes/Memories

Notes/Memories

Notes/Memories

Notes/Memories

Notes/Memories

Notes/Memories

Notes/Memories

Notes/Memories

Notes/Memories

Notes/Memories

Notes/Memories

Notes/Memories

Notes/Memories

Notes/Memories

Notes/Memories

Notes/Memories

Notes/Memories

Notes/Memories

Notes/Memories

Notes/Memories

Notes/Memories

Notes/Memories

Made in the USA
Las Vegas, NV
05 March 2024

86740394R00066